Usborne
Bedtime Stories
for Little Children

Usborne
Bedtime Stories
for Little Children

Contents

6

The Mouse's Wedding

Once upon a time, a family of mice
lived happily beside a stream. There was
Father Mouse, Mother Mouse and little Miss Mouse.

In no time at all, little Miss Mouse was all grown up.
"She needs a husband," thought Father Mouse, one day.

"Family trip!" he announced, the very next morning.
"The bags are packed. We're off on a journey
to find you a husband."

"You must have the best, most powerful husband in the whole world!" said Father Mouse as they set off.

"Really?" asked Miss Mouse.
"And who might that be?"

Father Mouse looked a little less sure.
"It's... it's... I know! It's the sun!" he said.

"He makes our days bright and warm.
He helps flowers to bloom and he ripens
the harvest fields. We'll ask him."

13

Father Mouse led the family up a snow-capped mountain.
All day long they climbed, until at last they reached the top.

The sun slipped slowly down
in the sky until he was close enough
to hear them.

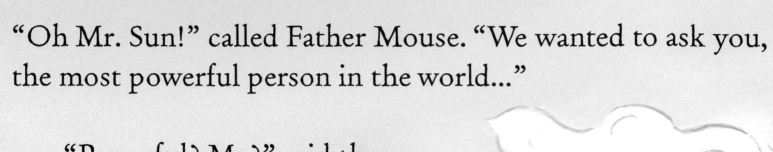

"Oh Mr. Sun!" called Father Mouse. "We wanted to ask you, the most powerful person in the world..."

"Powerful? Me?" said the sun.

"When that cloud covers my face, he blocks all my light and warmth. I'm not so powerful then."

"In that case," said Father Mouse, "we will talk to the cloud."

They clambered a little way down the mountain and slept until morning.

When they woke, they saw the cloud resting on the mountain top.

Father Mouse led the family back to the top.
"Mr. Cloud," he said politely. "We have been told
that you are the most powerful person in the world..."

"Powerful? Me?" said the cloud.

"When the wind blows, he bounces me all over the sky. I'm not so powerful then."

"In that case," said Father Mouse, "we will talk to the wind."

"Let's have breakfast first," said Mother Mouse.

Soon, the wind came along and puffed the cloud away.

"Mr. Wind! MR. WIND!" called Father Mouse. "We hear you're the most powerful person in the world..."

"Powerful? Me?" sighed the wind. "That wall can stop me in my tracks. I'm not so powerful then."

"In that case," began Father Mouse...

"Daddy, are we really going to talk to a wall?" asked Miss Mouse.

"Of course," said Father Mouse. "Mr. Wall, is it true that you're the most powerful being in the world?"

"I wish I was," said the wall sadly. "I tell you, I'm not even as powerful as a mouse."

"I may look strong," said the wall, "but I can feel a little
mouse nibbling at my bricks. At any moment, I could
come crashing down."

"Oh dear," said Father Mouse. "In that case, we will talk to the mouse."

"Yes please," said Miss Mouse.

Making their way along the wall, they found a young mouse.

"He's handsome!" thought Miss Mouse.

"Mr. Mouse," said Father Mouse. "We hear you're the most powerful person in the world..."

"I wouldn't say that,"
the mouse began.

"But you're more powerful than the wall,"
said Miss Mouse quickly.

"...and the wall is more powerful than the wind," added Mother Mouse.

"...and the wind is more powerful than the cloud," continued Father Mouse.

27

"...and the cloud is more powerful than the sun!" finished Miss Mouse triumphantly.

"Wow!" said the young mouse.

"I think you'd be the perfect husband for my daughter," said Father Mouse. "And it seems she likes you. Will you marry her?"

"I'd be delighted!" said the young mouse.

The two young mice
were married the very
next day, and all their
friends came to the
wedding...

...the sun
and the cloud
and the wind...

...though not all at once.

The Reluctant Dragon

One summer's evening long ago,
a shepherd raced down the hill to
his house. "Aaagghh!" he screamed.

34

He flung open the front door and burst inside. "I just saw a monster!" he panted.

It's as big as four horses!

"It has the longest, sharpest claws I've ever seen...

...a spiky tail like a dagger and shiny blue scales ALL OVER its body."

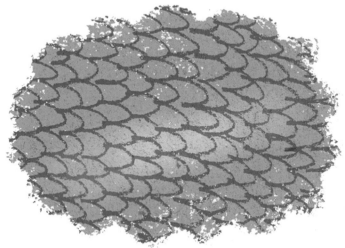

His son looked up from his book. "It sounds like a dragon, Dad," he said.

The boy had always wanted to meet a dragon.
"I wonder if it's friendly," he thought.

The next day, he set off
up the hill to find out.

Bye! See
you later.

39

The dragon *was* friendly. What's more, he was delighted to see the boy.

It's beautiful here but it does get lonely.

The boy smiled. He sat down and bombarded the dragon with questions, one after another.

The dragon told stories of long ago.

There were deadly,
fire-breathing dragons
at every turn.

And brave knights
fought them to rescue
grateful princesses.

As much as the dragon loved telling
stories, the boy loved hearing them.
He came back every day for more.

Then, one dreadful day, the villagers found out about the dragon. They were scared and that made them angry.

SLAY THE DRAGON!

BAN THE DRAGON

BANISH THE DRAGON!

NO DRAGON

SLAY THE DRAGON!

BAN THE DRAGON

The boy ran straight to the
dragon. "The villagers want
to get rid of you!"
he gasped.

But I wouldn't
hurt a fly!

That afternoon, the boy
heard even worse news.

He's coming!

Saint George,
the dragon
killer!

Who's
coming?

He's going to fight
the dragon!

The boy rushed back to the dragon.

"Saint George the dragon killer wants to fight you,"
cried the boy. "And he has the longest spear I've ever seen!"

But I don't like fighting.

"I'd better just hide in my cave until he goes away," said the dragon.

"You can't!" said the boy. "Everyone wants a fight!"

The dragon yawned.
"I'm sure you'll think
of something," he said.

The boy walked slowly back down to the village.

A crowd of villagers was telling George about the dangerous dragon.

He burned down five houses.

When the villagers had gone, the boy went up to Saint George.
"It's not true!" he said. "The dragon wouldn't hurt a fly."

"But everyone wants
a fight," said George.
"What can I do?"

"Follow me," said the boy.
And he took George to meet the dragon.

"I've had an idea," said the boy. "You can have a pretend fight." He turned to George. "Do you promise not to hurt him?"

"Well, it has to look real," said George.

But there'll be a feast after.

Hmm... Alright then.

The next morning, the entire village trekked up the hill to watch the fight.

The boy waited nervously by the dragon's cave.

Great cheers broke out when Saint George rode into view. But where was the dragon?

Then a roar echoed around the mountains.
Flames filled the air and the
dragon appeared.

His scales sparkled and he breathed out fire.
It was a magnificent sight.
The villagers took one look and fled.

"Charge!" yelled George.
He galloped forward, his
spear held high.

The dragon
bounded up.

And they shot
past each other.

"Missed!" roared
the crowd.

George and the dragon
lumbered around
and charged again.

This time, there was no way they could miss.

CLATTER! BANG! OUF!

The dragon gave a groan and slumped to the ground. George stood over him, triumphantly.

Cut off his head!

"I think the dragon has learned his lesson, don't you?" declared George. "Let's invite him to our feast."

And he led the villagers,
the boy and the dragon
back down the hill.

The feast went on until the stars came out. Everyone was happy.

The boy was happy because his plan had worked.

The villagers were happy because they'd seen a fight. George was happy because he'd won.

But the dragon was happiest of all.
He had lots of new friends...

...and a very full tummy.

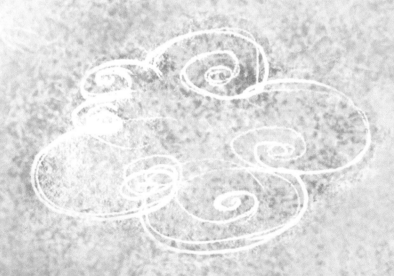

The Tortoise and the Eagle

It was a perfect summer
day in the orchard.

The sun shone and the wind
whispered softly in the trees.

But Tortoise
wasn't happy.

"Oh!" he sighed. "It's just
terrible being a tortoise."

His friends were puzzled.
"Why are you so glum?" they asked.

"You have a lovely log to sit on,
yummy apples to eat, and
a very shiny shell."

But Tortoise just mumbled and grumbled.

"Oh," he moaned, "it's terrible being me."

All day long,
he watched an
eagle in the sky.

She swooped down low...

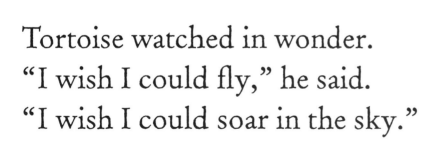

...and soared up high.
Her golden feathers
shimmered in the sun.

Tortoise watched in wonder.
"I wish I could fly," he said.
"I wish I could soar in the sky."

So he decided to try.

He closed his eyes, gritted his teeth, flapped his arms and hopped.

But he couldn't get into the sky.

"I know," said Tortoise,
"I need to start up high."
He clambered onto a rock...

jumped into
the air...

...and landed
SPLOSH on the
soggy grass.

OOF!

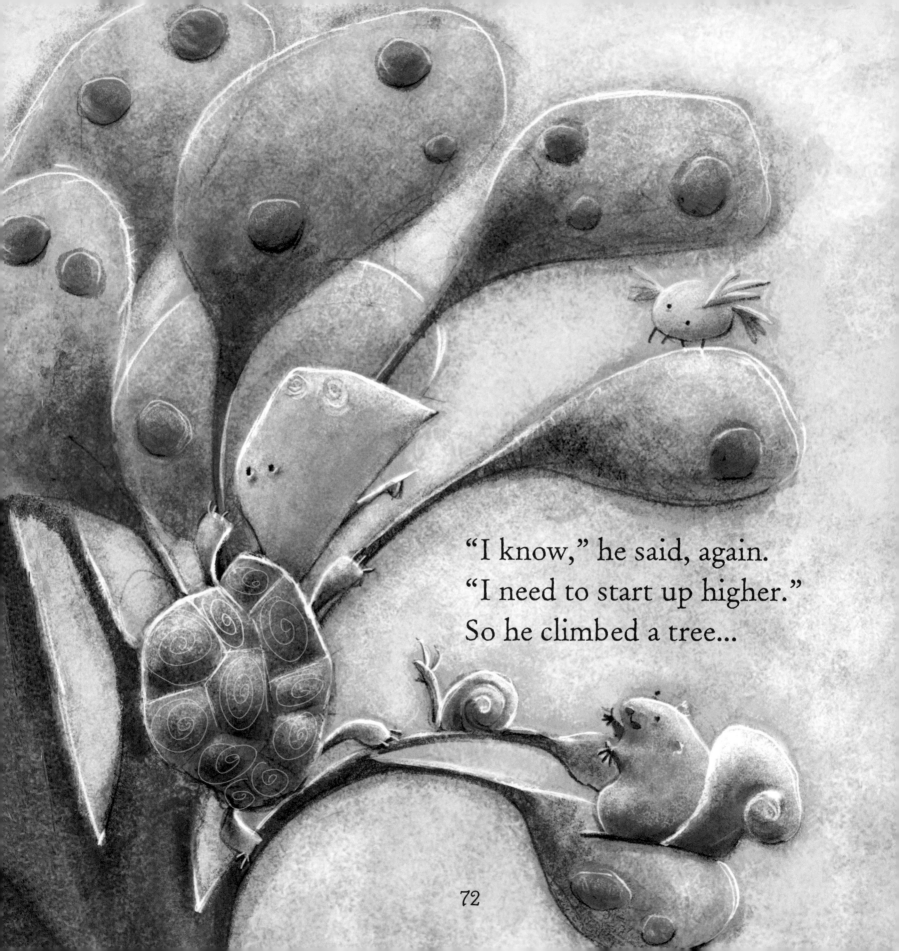

"I know," he said, again.
"I need to start up higher."
So he climbed a tree...

flung himself
off...

...and landed SPLAT!
in a muddy puddle.

He called to the eagle up above.

"Eagle! Eagle! Flying so high.
Won't you take me into the sky?"

The golden bird
swooped down
from the clouds.

"Little tortoise," she
squawked, "why do
you wish to fly?"

Tortoise puffed up his
chest and answered proudly.
"So I can be just like you."

"I'll give you my log to rest on," said Tortoise. "And you can have my juicy apples to eat."

"Very well," said the eagle.
"I will take you into the sky."

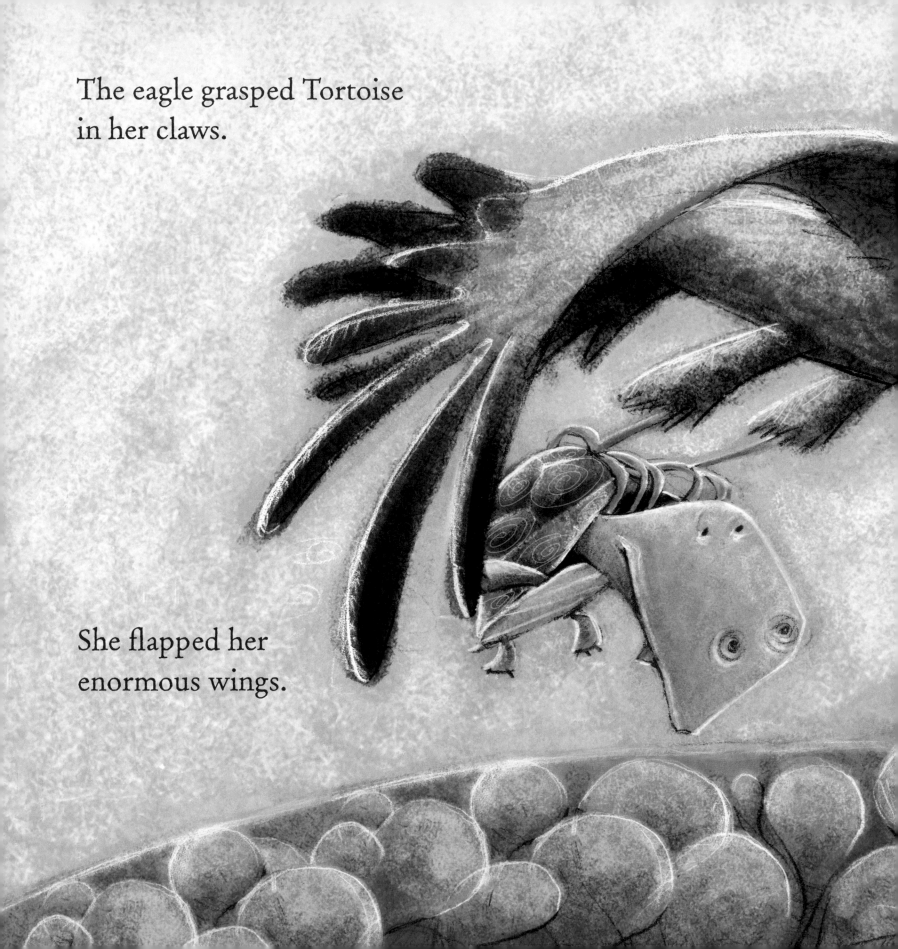

The eagle grasped Tortoise
in her claws.

She flapped her
enormous wings.

Up and up they rose,
up through the clouds
to the bright blue sky.

The wind tickled
Tortoise's face.
"I'm flying," he
laughed.

They rose higher
and higher. Below
them, the trees
looked tiny.

The tortoise gazed at the ground.
It was a VERY long way down.

His head felt dizzy.
His tummy went wobbly.
And then he started to cry.

"Eagle! Eagle! Take me
down! I don't like it up
in the sky!"

The eagle carried the tortoise
back to the ground.

"Little tortoise," she said.
"You have no feathers. You have no wings."

"You are not made for flying.
Keep your apples and your log.
Be happy with who you are."

Tortoise watched the eagle
soar up to the sky.

He munched his apples.
He sat on his log. And he
no longer wanted to fly.

"It's terrific being a tortoise," he said.

The
Ant
and the
Grasshopper

It was a glorious summer's day.
Grasshopper sang in the sun.

Ant was working.
He huffed...
and he puffed...
and he g-r-o-a-n-ed...

as he gathered food
for his winter store.

Grasshopper grinned.
He lay back and enjoyed
the sun on his face.

"I'm bored," said Grasshopper,
after a while. "Play with me, Ant?"

"Sorry Grasshopper,
I can't," said Ant.
"There's too much to do."

93

"I need to collect food
and then to make a
home for the winter."

94

"But winter is months away.
Enjoy the sun with me
while you can!"

"Winter may be months away," said Ant,
"but it will come – and all too quickly.

If you don't work now... Well, when the sun has long gone and the earth is sleeping, you will be cold and hungry."

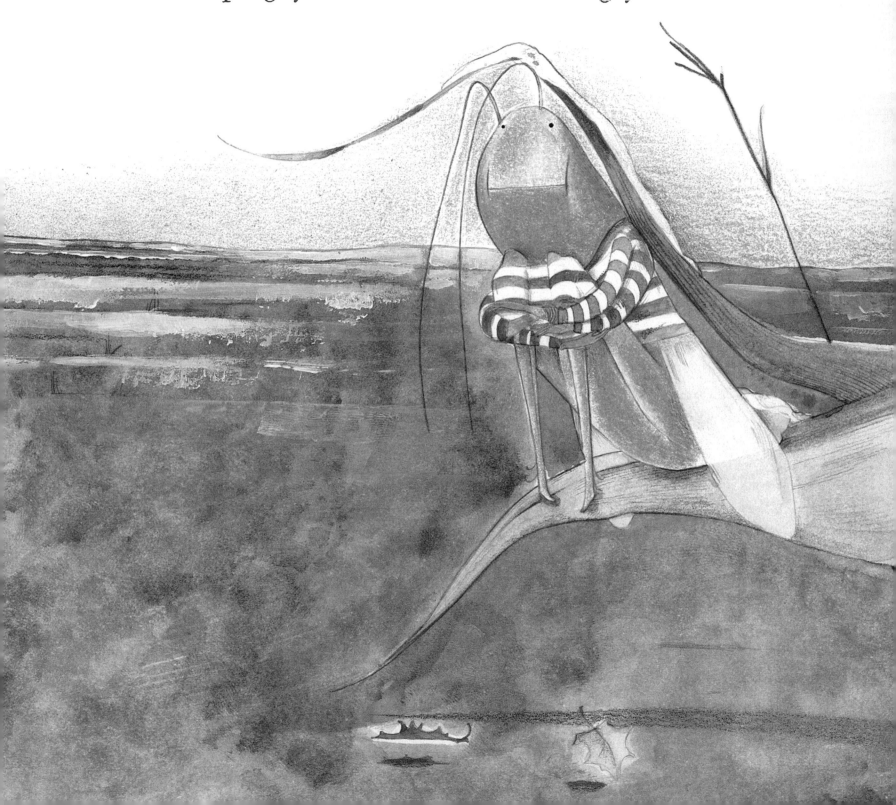

Grasshopper simply laughed and continued to sing.

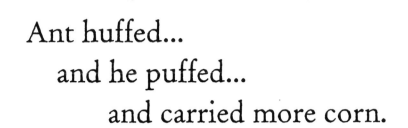

Ant huffed...
and he puffed...
and carried more corn.

Sure enough, winter came.
The trees stood bare against the bleak sky.
Snow dusted the fields.

Tucked up snug in his little home, Ant looked at his food store and smiled.

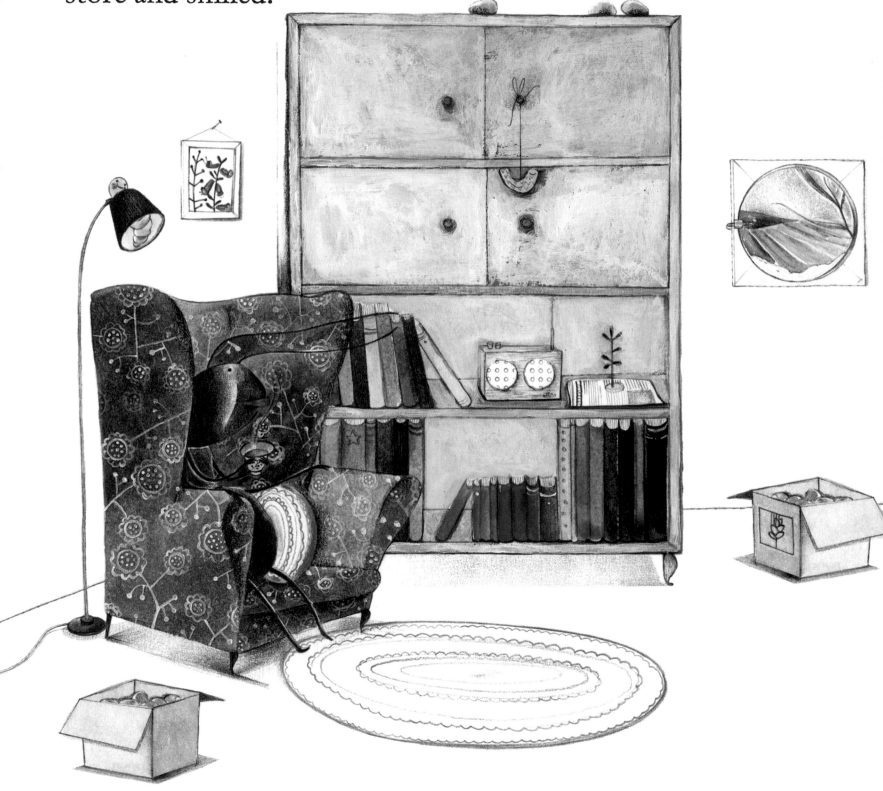

He had boxes galore, plenty to keep
him fed until the spring buds blossomed.

Grasshopper scrunched himself
up outside, trying to find
shelter under a leaf.

But the wind blew through his shivering
body, however tightly he curled up.
His tummy growled with hunger.

At last, he fought through the wind to knock on Ant's door.

"Grasshopper, you look frozen!" Ant cried. "Come inside and warm up."

"Th-th-thank you," shivered Grasshopper,
his teeth chattering in the cold.

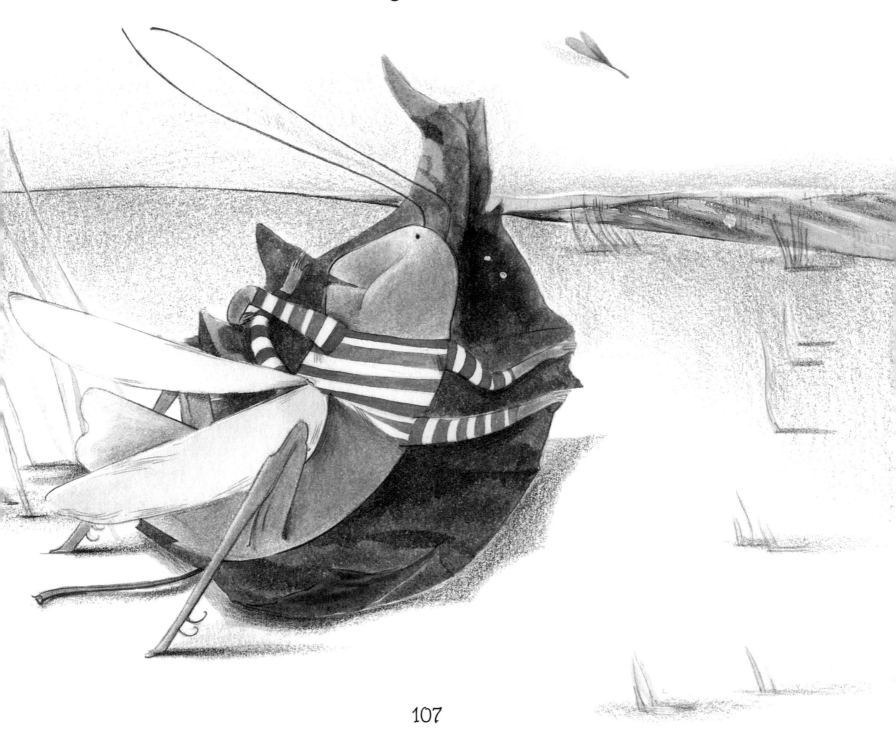

"Warm yourself by the stove," said Ant, "and I'll make supper."

Grasshopper beamed at
the thought. He could almost
taste the toasted corn already.

"Thank you, dear, clever
Ant," said Grasshopper, as he
basked in the warmth of the flames.
"Next summer I'll work too!"

The Owl
and the
Pussycat

The Owl and the Pussycat went to sea
in a beautiful pea-green boat.

They took some honey
and plenty of money,

wrapped up in a
five pound note.

The Owl looked up to
the stars above and sang
to a small guitar.

Oh lovely Pussy!
Oh Pussy my love...

What a beautiful
Pussy you are, you are,

what a beautiful
Pussy you are.

Pussy said to the Owl,
"You elegant fowl,

how charmingly
sweet you sing."

119

"Oh let us be married — too long we have tarried."

"But what shall we do for a ring?"

They sailed away...

...for a year and a day,

to the land where the Bong-tree grows.

And there in the wood a Piggy-wig stood,
     with a ring at the end of his nose, his nose,

with a ring at the
end of his nose.

"Dear Pig,
are you willing,

to sell for one shilling,
your ring?"

Said the Piggy, "I will!"

127

So they took it away,

and were married
next day,

by the turkey who
lives on the hill.

129

They dined on mince, and slices of quince,

which they ate with a runcible spoon.

And hand in hand,
on the edge of the sand,

they danced by the
light of the moon,

the moon,

they danced by the
light of the moon.

About the Authors

Aesop

Two of the stories in this book were taken from Aesop's Fables.
These fables are a collection of short stories, first told in
ancient Greece around 4,000 years ago. Nobody knows exactly
who Aesop was – he might have been a wealthy man or he might
have been a slave – but his stories have always been popular.
Today, they are known all around the world.
The stories are often about animals and they always have
a "moral" (a message or lesson) at the end.
The moral in "The Tortoise and the Eagle" is
be happy with who you are.
The moral in "The Ant and the Grasshopper" is be prepared!